Possession in Session

E.J. RUSSELL

Cover art: L.C. Chase, http://lcchase.com
Proofreading: Hana Katen, Meg DesCamp

ISBN: 978-1-947033-97-9

First ebook edition
June 2019
First print edition
July 2024

Contact information:
ejr@ejrussell.com

Possession in Session

E.J. RUSSELL

For everyone who's ever had that "OMG! I'm naked at school!" dream.

ABOUT

Possession in Session takes place in the Mythmatched story universe that begins with *Cutie and the Beast*. It occurs between the events in *Demon on the Down-Low* and *Witch Under Wraps*, and, although a couple of characters from the previous books are mentioned, can be read as a stand-alone.

Chapter One

Wash Hernández raised a hand to the nurse at the ER admitting desk. "See you tomorrow, Brenda."

"'Night, Wash." She wrinkled her nose. "Killer shift, eh?"

"No kidding." Wash rolled his shoulders and cracked his neck. A frost giant with explosive diarrhea made for a very... *odoriferous* afternoon. *If anybody ever wonders what a shit slushie looks—and smells—like, I can give them an up close and personal description.*

Thank the triple goddess that United Memorial had staff showers. Wash had taken three before he'd felt decontaminated enough to raid the supply closet for fresh scrubs and venture back into the wards.

But cleanup was his job, and better him than the nurses or doctors. Although as he'd watched them deal with the poor, miserable giant, he'd felt a wistful pang that he'd never rise above orderly. When he was a kid, he'd wanted nothing more than to be a nurse or paramedic. He'd aced every biology class in high school. Afterward, he'd totally *smoked* the human EMT training program, so he'd be ready when his familiar chose him and he could finally tackle the spellcraft side of the training.

That was fifteen years ago. Back then, he'd still believed a familiar *would* choose him, even though his *calon*, the organ that marked him as a supernatural entity—aka supe —had a congenital irregularity. He'd attended dozens of Pairing ceremonies over the years, every time a familiar presented itself to the Portland witches' collective. None had ever picked him, and when he'd turned thirty, he'd aged out of Pairing eligibility. Since male witches couldn't perform even basic spells without a familiar to act as their intermediary to the triple goddess, when it came to magic, he was as null as the average human.

Guess no familiar could get past my "irregularity."

As an orderly, though, he could still be part of a supe healthcare team, even if he wasn't providing direct medical/magical care.

"Besides," he murmured as he strode down the corridor toward the staff locker room, "*somebody* has to clean up the shit."

He swiped his badge through the card reader, and as he was opening the door, metal rattled and *clished* from around the next corner. He let the door *whoosh* shut.

"Hello? Somebody need help?" No answer, but he heard a thud as if something heavy had hit the wall. He hurried down the hall. "Take it easy. I'm coming. I—*whoa there!*"

A rolling cart lay on its side in the middle of the corridor, one wheel spinning. What looked like an entire ER's worth of metal implements littered the gray industrial carpet, but that wasn't the most astonishing thing in the hallway.

Nope. That would be the big naked dude—the big naked winged dude—blundering down the hallway with both hands over his eyes.

"Hey, buddy. Hold on there."

The guy's head shot up, and he dropped his hands. Although he was squinting, red light spilled from his eyes, his eyelashes casting shadows on his wide cheeks. "I'd forgotten how *bright* the Upper World is," he moaned.

Okay. Black, leathery wings. Light sensitivity. Glowing red irises. "Demon, right? Where's your eye protection?"

"Eye protection?" The guy shielded his face with one hand. "I'm sorry. I didn't know—"

"Hey, it's okay. I heard the Supe Med Tech program was getting a new student from the Host. You must be him." The demon nodded miserably but didn't drop his hand. "You're kinda in the wrong spot, though, buddy. We try to keep the nudity to a minimum, at least for staff and students. Where's your stuff? I can help you get up to the dorms. I'm Wash, by the way."

"Stuff?"

"You know. Your bags. Your clothes. Your supplies. You got the list, right?"

"List?" The guy's wings drooped. "There's a list?"

"Yeah. All students are supposed to arrive with five sets of scrubs, two sets of bed linens, a— You know what? Screw it. Come with me." Wash turned back the way he'd come, but he'd only gone a couple of steps before he realized the demon wasn't following. *He can't see, you blockhead.* He approached the demon slowly, not wanting to startle him. "I'm gonna take your arm. That okay?"

The demon's wings drooped even more. "You don't mind touching a demon?"

"I've touched worse things today, trust me." He grasped the demon's biceps—*hmmm, nice muscles*—and led him down the hall. The guy's brown skin was warm under Wash's palm, and *whoops*. His wings nearly took out a wall-mounted fire extinguisher. "Maybe pull the wings in a bit?"

"Oh. Of course." He furled his wings, and they disappeared under little flaps of skin on his shoulders—then the flaps themselves smoothed over to resemble burn scars.

"Does that hurt? Wing deployment and retraction?"

"Not really. The light is much more uncomfortable."

Wash winced. "Right. We're almost there." He paused outside the supply room door. "By the way, what's your name?"

The demon hunched his shoulders, and Wash figured if the wings had still been on display, they'd have drooped all the way to the floor. "If you don't mind, I'd, um, rather not say."

Wash blinked. "Oookay. But we'll need to call you something. Put something other than *Demon Dude* on your name tag. What about initials? Will that work?"

He nodded hesitantly. "Y-yes." Then his eyes lit up—literally—and his shoulders squared as if he'd just thrown off a massive weight. "Here in the Upper World, I shall be known as AJ."

"AJ. Got it." Wash swiped his badge and opened the door. "Well, AJ, welcome to my world."

"The Upper World, you mean?"

"Nah. I mean the world of a St. Stupid's orderly."

"St. Stupid's? But I thought this was United Memorial." Poor AJ sounded positively bewildered.

Wash chuckled. "It is. But United Memorial is what you might call a dual-purpose hospital. One side is for humans. The other side is for supes—although the humans don't know that. We call the supe side St. Stupid's."

AJ sighed. "I have much to learn," he said humbly.

"Don't worry about it. I've worked here for twelve years, so if you need anything, just come to me. If I don't know the answer myself, I'll know how to get it. Wait here." Wash positioned AJ next to the wall and headed to the far corner of the supply closet, which was a lot farther away than the footprint of St. Stupid's would lead anyone to believe. *That's right. It pays to have witches on staff who know their stuff.* Folding space wasn't only good for translocation between fixed endpoints: It rocked when it came to increasing square footage for storage.

"Aha!" The unopened box of bespelled spectacles was exactly where Wash remembered. The hospital had started stocking supplies for demons after the Realm Accords passed. As Wash understood it, an unspecified number of demons would be mainstreaming into the supernatural community over the next months as the new protocols went into effect. How cool that St. Stupid's got one of the first!

He studied the glasses in the box. *Whoa.* Demons must come in all sizes, because some of these things were big enough for a trow while others would fit a pixie.

Wash picked out a nice pair of nerdtastic horn-rims that would look great on AJ's classic features. *I wonder if all demons are that good-looking. Not to mention built.* AJ had to be six-three, same as Wash, and everything looked to be perfectly, er, in proportion. *Sue me. I looked. I'm a gay witch. But I'm not a perv, so no ogling the hot naked demon dude.*

He hurried over and placed the glasses in AJ's hand. "Here. Put these on. The spell will adjust for the light, even the dreaded hospital fluorescents."

"Th-thanks." AJ fumbled the glasses onto his face and blinked. The red glow died, leaving his eyes a deep, rich brown, and wonder suffused his face. "Oh. You're so beautiful. Are you an angel?"

Heat rushed up Wash's throat. "Me? I'm nothing special." He turned resolutely away from the admiration in AJ's eyes. *He's just grateful that he's not still playing blind-man's-bumper-cars in the hallway.* "Let's get you some scrubs and sheets, and I'll take you up to the dorms."

AJ followed him a little closely, making Wash wonder if demons had issues with personal space. Wash ordered his very interested dick to stand down.

"Here." Wash handed AJ a set of standard blue scrubs. "You're about my size, so these ought to fit." He eyed AJ's bare feet—*geez, even his feet are gorgeous*—and added a pair of canvas boat shoes. "Put all that on and we'll get everything else squared away."

AJ nodded and smiled shyly. "I've never worn clothes before in my own body."

"You've, er, worn them on somebody else's body?"

"Well, I've worn other people's bodies. They had the clothes."

"You mean you… you…"

"Possessed people? Yes." AJ paused with his hands on the drawstring of his scrub pants. "Does that make you uncomfortable? Would you rather I leave?"

"No." Wash shook himself like a werewolf shedding water. "It was just… a surprise. That's all."

"I wouldn't blame you, you know." AJ's eyes were so sad Wash wanted to weep. "Even other demons don't want to be near me."

"Why? Do they object to possession? I thought that was kind of a demon thing."

"Oh, they don't object to possession per se. But I wasn't doing it for my own amusement. I was summoned. Bound."

Anger bloomed in Wash's chest. "Enslaved, you mean."

AJ nodded, but didn't meet Wash's eyes, focused instead on smoothing his shirt over his chest. "An alchemist in 1283 discovered my true name and summoned me into a warded circle. I was passed down from magician to magician, from master to apprentice, for centuries, possessing humans whenever my current master commanded." AJ peeked up at Wash from under his eyebrows. "Other demons consider me unlucky. They were glad to get rid of me."

"Well, *screw* 'em. It's not easy to get accepted into the SMT program here at St. Stupid's. I've *never* heard of them admitting anybody mid-term, so if you're here now, you're obviously something special."

The swoop of the elevator's ascent was reminiscent of summoning dislocation syndrome and sent dread skating across Auni-jel-Chandu's skin under the fabric of his unaccustomed clothing. *No one knows my true name here. To them, I am not Auni-jel-Chandu but AJ. I will never again be summoned into a restraining circle. I'm free.*

The thought made him breathe marginally easier, although he still wasn't used to the scents of the hospital: disinfectant, antibacterial soap, plastics. But overlaying all of that, alluring and nearly hypnotic, was the aroma of citrus and mint wafting off Wash's skin.

"I apologize for being so unprepared. I'm afraid I wasn't given many instructions." And he was used to instructions. Minute, explicit, *extensive* instructions. Everyone knew that when interacting with demons, allowing any leeway led to death and untold destruction.

Literally.

Wash grinned at him, a flash of very white teeth against skin a shade or two lighter than AJ's own. AJ was interested to note that one of his incisors overlapped its neighbor. The tiny flaw, and Wash's lack of concern over displaying it, reassured him. Every one of AJ's string of magician masters had been obsessed with the pursuit of perfection, whether of person, property, or existence. Not one had ever felt they'd achieved *enough*.

"Don't worry about it. Everybody's new at least once, am I right?" The elevator pinged, and its doors slid open onto a mercifully dim corridor. "This is the dorm level for students, but I think you'll be the only one here."

AJ's hands trembled, and he wiped them on the rough cotton of his pants. "I'm the only student?"

Wash laughed. "Hardly. There are about a dozen others, but only first-semester students are required to live on-site. After that, they want to put some distance between where they work and where they live, so as soon as they pass their first exams, they move out into the city." He glanced at AJ. "Once you get your feet under you, you might want to do the same."

AJ shuddered. Living on his own among humans, without even the structure of the hospital, its classes and assigned duties? *No. Not yet. Maybe not ever.* "Are we required to move out?"

"Nope. You can live up here through your entire program if you want. Just, you know, wanted you to get that you'll have other options. I mean, it's not much." He threw open the door to a room painted a cool blue, the same color as his scrubs.

AJ stepped inside. The blinds were drawn on the single large window, but sunlight striped the carpet where it bled through the slats. A squat table topped by a gooseneck lamp stood next to the single bed in the corner. In the opposite corner was a plain pine dresser, a sink with a mirror mounted above it, and a narrow closet with a mended handle. "It's wonderful."

"Wonderful?" Wash winced. "I, ah, guess that compared to Sheol— I mean, I've heard stories, yeah? We all have. Stories about the conditions down there made the rounds after the Accords passed and the renovations started."

"Sheol… well, yes, it has its issues. But I was far more comfortable there than trapped in an ensorcelled jewel in a magician's workroom." Especially since nobody in Sheol had come anywhere near him lately.

"Man, that sucks." Wash gripped AJ's shoulder, and for some reason, that simple touch—one of comfort, not coercion—untangled the knot of anxiety in AJ's belly. "If you ever need to talk about anything, just hit me up."

"Thank you. But I've been working with a therapist for a while now. That's how I ended up in this program. He gave me some aptitude tests."

"Therapist? You don't mean Dr. Kendrick, do you? Big fae dude?"

"Yes. You know him?"

"*Everybody* knows Dr. Kendrick. Especially if we've got council-ordered treatment of our own."

"And do you? Have council ordered treatment?" At the flare of pain in Wash's lovely brown eyes, AJ held up his hands. "Not that you have to tell me anything. I'm sorry. I haven't had a lot of experience in interpersonal relationships that didn't involve torture and maiming, so —"

"Nah, it's okay. All supes who can't fully manifest their abilities—shifters who can't shift, dryads with plant allergies, witches who can't do spellcraft, that kind of thing—we all have to meet with Dr. Kendrick on the regular so we don't suddenly go off the rails."

"Which one are you?"

"Witch. Something's off with my *calon*, has been since birth. They think that's why I was never able to bond with a familiar. And all male witches have to bond with a familiar to act as our intermediary to the triple goddess or we can't do spellcraft worth shit." Wash grinned, but there was an edge to it, a sadness, a bitterness that he couldn't quite hide. "That's why I'll never be admitted into the SMT program myself. I could handle the mundane medical part, no problem. But I can't pass the magical exams."

Daring, AJ placed his hand—carefully claw-free—on Wash's arm. "I'm sorry. That is, if this is something you really want to do."

Wash grinned wryly. "I'd give just about anything to be where you are."

AJ snatched his hand away, a chill racing down his spine and making his shoulders twitch with the urge to extend his wings and fly away. If this had been the old days, before the Realm Accords, and if he'd been a demon rated for soul collection, Wash's revelation would have been the opening for negotiations: his heart's desire now in exchange for an eternity fueling the Sheol boilers whenever the overlords decided to call in the debt. In AJ's own deplorable history, he'd have been required to report the news to his magician master—whoever it happened to be at the time.

Wash seemed to realize he'd crossed some kind of line, even if the line didn't exist anymore. He ran a hand through his hair—something AJ had been wishing he could do himself because it was just so dark and shiny and *soft*-looking. "Well, I better be heading out. Got an early shift tomorrow." He pointed to the desk where a tower of large books teetered next to a shorter stack of paperbacks. "Looks like they at least dropped off your textbooks. Classes start at nine." He jerked his thumb over his shoulder. "Bathroom's down the hall. Cafeteria's on the second floor. It's, um, been nice to meet you."

"Nice to meet you too." AJ couldn't help the thread of wistfulness in his tone. Other than Dr. Kendrick, whose job it was to be sympathetic, nobody had ever been kind to him before, let alone helpful.

Wash lifted a hand in farewell and walked back toward the elevator, whistling tunelessly. AJ stood in the doorway, admiring the way Wash's broad shoulders moved under the scrubs, the way his back veed into his narrow hips, the way his posterior flexed with his confident stride.

An odd sensation stirred in AJ's groin, and he glanced down. *Beelzebub's horns! Is that a... a...* He closed the door quickly and leaned against it, staring down at the way his pants were distended. His progenitor had given him male genitalia, but AJ had never realized they were this *functional. It's so... so* indiscreet. *How do incubi cope?*

Dr. Kendrick had been very concerned about the ways AJ had been coerced, the things he'd been forced to endure, the horrible acts he'd been forced to perform. Apparently AJ had been lucky in one respect at least: His magician masters had all sought power through riches and influence and shameful secrets. None of them had ever forced AJ to either submit to or execute a sex act.

The demon who'd manifested him, his Sheol progenitor, wasn't interested in sex at all, except as information contained in a rare volume, and then he cared more about owning the book than engaging in the practices it described.

I'm a fifteen hundred-year-old virgin. But considering the *other* things he'd been forced to do and to endure, that was probably the best possible outcome of his centuries of servitude.

Alone in the sterile room, cool air from a vent in the ceiling tickling his skin and raising gooseflesh, his first ever erection subsided. He sank onto the narrow bunk. *What am I doing here?* He still couldn't believe this hadn't been some mistake. How could anyone—let alone the supe council—trust him in the Upper World with no monitor, no anchor? Didn't they remember what he'd done? The hundreds of possessions over the centuries? Granted, he'd had no choice. A conjured demon had no option but to acquiesce when the mage who held his name made demands, no matter how heinous.

But the last possession—the *murder*—that had been all on him, and he didn't regret it. He'd do it again, if he had the opportunity, because that necromancer had been truly evil. *And it was his own fault for not setting the wards on me properly.* So AJ had possessed his own master. He'd burned every scroll with his name on it to ash. Slagged the drives of every computer. Wiped every file from the cloud.

And then he'd stabbed the vile body—with himself still inside—in the heart.

Yes, it was agonizing. Yes, AJ felt the pain. Yes, AJ experienced the death, just as he always did when death was the goal of a possession. AJ thought he'd die too, along with his last master. Dissipate into merciful nothingness. But instead, he'd tumbled back to Sheol, much to the horror of his progenitor and every other demon he encountered.

After all, any demon who'd been summoned, who'd been at the beck and call of not one, but dozens of alchemists, wizards, and necromancers over the centuries, was *de facto* a disgrace. Anathema. Tainted. They'd avoided him as if he might infect them with his ill-luck.

AJ sighed and stood up, studying the bare mattress and the stack of bedding at its foot. He'd never had a mattress before, let alone sheets. He'd possessed a chambermaid once, though, back in 1837, so he was able to draw on her experience—although the sheet with the elasticized corners perplexed him until he realized they fit over the corners of the mattress. *Ingenious.* He had so much to learn.

A paper with his schedule of classes sat next to the books on the desk. He touched the frames of his glasses, gratitude warming him from the inside out. How kind, how thoughtful, of Wash to make sure AJ could not only see, but would be comfortable navigating this highly illuminated world, even though AJ was granted an opportunity that Wash desired but could never have.

He owed it to Wash, to Dr. Kendrick, to the people who'd fought so hard to break Sheol's chains, not to squander this chance.

So he picked up the first book, sat down on the bed—*so soft!*—and began to read.

Chapter Two

Wash's dreams last night had been populated by tall, winged men with infinitely sad dark eyes, smooth brown skin, and curly black hair. And no, they—or rather *he*, because it was always the same guy—hadn't always been naked. Although Wash hadn't objected when he was. Because the scenery was spectacular.

Since there was no point in trying to get back to sleep after the last dream—one of the naked ones—he gave up, showered, and headed in for his shift a good hour and a half early. He could pretend it was to double-check the stock rooms, but why bother? He was on his way to AJ, and he knew it. It was only a friendly gesture, right? The geography of St. Stupid's was challenging, since it wasn't restricted to a single dimension, so AJ could get lost on his way to class and wander around for hours. Days. *Weeks.*

Really, it would be irresponsible of Wash *not* to check in on him. After all, wasn't it an orderly's job to help out anybody in need? He was being proactive, damn it.

So he keyed himself into the staff entrance, waved at the matronly werewolf at the security station, and headed upstairs to the cafeteria. It was pretty empty this early—a couple of bleary-eyed nurses grabbing breakfast before heading home, two doctors deep in conversation by the window, an orderly with a thousand-yard stare downing a giant cup of coffee. *Huh. Maybe the frost giant is still having, er, explosions.*

Wash nodded to the green-skinned bauchan carrying a chafing dish nearly as large as their torso. The cafeteria food had taken a marked turn for the incredible after St. Stupid's followed Dr. Kendrick's advice and hired the brownie who'd been the lead cook for the Unseelie King. The Realm Accords hadn't only benefited demons. Fae were venturing out of Faerie again, although if they weren't human-appearing, they had to keep to supe-only venues like St. Stupid's so as not to violate the Secrecy Pact and reveal supe presence to humans.

Witches were lucky there—they weren't restricted to supe spaces, since they looked fully human. Well, they *were* fully human, technically. They were just human *plus*. Enough witch DNA had gotten spread around over the years that a recessive gene could get activated and produce a child with a *calon*, even if both parents were magic-null. Confused the hells out of them when their kid started manifesting weird stuff before it could even talk.

That's why Wash's adoptive brother Ky had ended up at the orphanage, although Wash had been plopped there for the opposite reason: He *didn't* manifest any weird stuff. Thank goodness their *brujo* dads had fostered and then adopted them before they'd gotten too screwed up.

He grabbed a coffee from the perpetual service in the corner, pretending that was the only reason he was here, and not because he was scoping out the place in search of a certain demon. He nodded at the other orderly who seemed mesmerized by the stir-stick holder.

"Hey," Wash said as he added a dollop of cream to his cup. "Rough shift?"

The other guy jerked, his throat working. "Frost giant," he croaked.

"Say no more." Wash saluted him with his cup. "Been there." *And sounds like I'll be there again.* But for now, he had another goal. *Find AJ.* He strolled out of the cafeteria and headed to the elevator. He might as well start his search from the top and work down.

When he stepped out on the dorm floor, the silence was almost eerie, causing the skin on his lower back to prickle. Had it felt the same way yesterday? He increased his pace, his coffee sloshing in the cup. Would AJ have gotten a similar weird feeling, being the only person on the floor? *Damn it, I should have taken a little more time to acclimate him, introduce him around.* Although the staff on the late shifts— the staff on any shift, for that matter—didn't have a lot of time to spare, they'd at least have made AJ welcome.

He knocked on the door and called, "AJ? It's Wash."

The door flew open and AJ was right *there,* all six foot *more* of him in fresh scrubs, his cute hipster glasses perched on his nose. "Hello. I didn't expect to see you this morning."

"Well, you know." Wash brandished his cup. "Just fueling up before my shift. Thought I'd see how you were doing. Make sure you found the classroom okay. Have you already eaten?"

AJ blinked, his brow knotting as if the question confused him. "N-no. I've been, er, reading. You know. Textbooks."

Wash grinned. "Well, I hope you snuck a few snacks back up here with you after dinner last night."

AJ bit his lip. "Dinner?"

Wash's jaw dropped. "You mean you didn't eat last night either?"

"No. Is that wrong? Will I be punished?"

"Of course not, but students have a daily meal allowance in the cafeteria, although that means you have to eat, you know, *in* the cafeteria. In the past, students have tried to persuade the program administrators that they should get a per diem to eat at restaurants out in the city—not that they were successful. But the food here is really good now."

AJ ducked his head. "I'm sorry. It didn't occur to me. I'm not used to eating. Demons don't, as a rule. We don't need food in order to survive, and minions aren't allowed to without their master's permission."

This time, Wash's jaw nearly hit the floor. "You've *never* eaten? At all? *Ever*? Not even when you were, you know, in possession?"

"Magician masters aren't any more benevolent than demon overlords. Depriving the possessed subject of food proves to both the demon and the victim who is in control."

Anger burned behind Wash's eyes. "You don't have *masters* or *overlords* anymore. The only person who controls you is *you*."

AJ tilted his head, as if he were weighing Wash's words against some internal metric. "But that's not entirely true, is it? I am here at the whim of the supe council. They could order me back to Sheol if I'm unsatisfactory. The instructors here could do the same if my performance doesn't meet their standards."

Wash frowned. AJ had a point. "Everybody has expectations to fulfill. I mean, if I screw up on the job, I could get fired, just like you could get expelled from the program if you fail all your exams. But the folks with authority are subject to rules too. If anyone—student or teacher, boss or employee—breaks those rules or doesn't meet those expectations, then the consequences are on them personally."

AJ's eyebrows rose. "Ah. Natural consequences. I understand witches are quite committed to those."

"Well, yeah. I mean, isn't everybody?"

"No. My magician masters did their utmost to assure that they'd never incur the consequences of their actions." He smiled wryly. "They had me for that. I did the dirty work, so they could evade on a technicality."

Wash's heart jolted—whether in sympathy or horror, he wasn't sure, nor was he sure it mattered. "Did you *want* to do the dirty work?"

AJ's full lips parted, his chest rising in a quick breath. "Nobody ever asked—" He shook his head decisively. "No. I never did."

Wash grinned, relief sweeping through him. "Good. Then what do you say we grab some breakfast? Better take advantage of it now, while you're still just sitting in lectures. Once you get to the clinical practicums, I hear that eating first is not such a great idea."

AJ tried to focus on Wash's cheerful chatter as they navigated a confusing maze of hallways, some of which he was certain they traversed twice. But with his belly writhing like a basket of pit vipers, he wasn't certain he could trust his senses.

My first class. My first time interacting with others in the Upper World while unbound. He glanced sidelong at Wash. *Not* precisely *my first time.* If the others were like Wash, perhaps AJ could manage, even excel, in this new life.

Wash stopped in a wide archway, gesturing to the enormous room beyond. "Voila. The St. Stupid's cafeteria. We're in luck. It's pretty empty this early."

"Empty?" To AJ's eyes, it was cluttered with an excessive number of tables and chairs and populated with more people than he'd ever been near. *In my own body anyway.*

"What would you like for your first meal ever?" Wash closed his eyes and inhaled. "Mmmm. Smell that bacon?"

AJ sniffed experimentally. *Singed flesh.* He pressed his hand to his mouth and backed away until his shoulders hit the wall opposite the door.

Wash hurried over to him. "Are you okay?"

AJ swallowed twice, fighting nausea. "Perhaps I should wait until later. Too many new experiences in one day..."

"Right. Sorry." Wash took AJ's elbow and led him around a corner and into an alcove with windows overlooking a courtyard. He eased AJ onto a padded bench. "Wait here. I'll be right back."

AJ gazed at the trees below, their leaves fluttering in an unseen breeze. Did they mind, those trees, enclosed as they were by glass and brick, with concrete under their branches instead of earth? Did they yearn for the company of others of their kind, or for the anonymity of the forest?

A woman in green scrubs, her brown hair loose around her shoulders, stepped into the courtyard and crossed to a maple. She wrapped her arms around its trunk—and vanished, her scrubs crumpling to the ground, as if the tree had welcomed her inside.

Dryad. AJ sighed. So the trees had a champion after all. *Good.*

"Here you go."

AJ startled at the voice at his back, heart bucking until he remembered. *It's only Wash. My days of looking over my shoulder are over.* He glanced up into Wash's worried face. "I'm sorry. I was woolgathering."

Wash handed him a steaming cardboard cup. "Try this. It's herbal tea. I didn't want to ply you with coffee, since it's kinda an acquired taste, and caffeine's effects—"

"Temporary increase in alertness, heart rate, and blood pressure. An excess may cause jitteriness, confusion, and diarrhea."

Wash winced. "Uh. Yeah. Right. Anyway, the tea's chamomile. It's supposed to be—"

"Calming," they said in unison.

AJ smiled apologetically. "I read about both in *Pharmaceuticals: Natural, Chemical, and Magical* last night."

"Hitting the textbooks already, huh? You're gonna rock this joint."

"I don't think so. I'm not rated for apocalyptical events." He inhaled the tea's aroma. *Subtle, and so very far from the stench of sulfur.* He took a sip. *Oh.* The flavor was equally distant from brimstone dust, the only thing that had ever touched his tongue before. And while AJ was more than familiar with excessive heat on his *skin*, he'd never experienced it on the *inside*. He closed his eyes to savor the unaccustomed sensations. "Thank you," he murmured. *It seems I have a champion as well.* The thought warmed him more than the tea.

"You're welcome."

AJ felt Wash settle beside him on the bench and opened his eyes. "Wash. That's an unusual name, isn't it?"

Wash stared down into his coffee. "I started out at an orphanage, and the folks who ran the place weren't big on imagination. They named all the kids after states. My full name is Washington. My brother Ky's is Kentucky." He shrugged. "I mean, it was okay for the two of us, and for Florida, Montana, and Virginia. But poor New Hampshire and Rhode Island had a terrible time."

"I suppose I shouldn't cast stones. Demon names aren't precisely mundane. But that's because we don't want to risk any unscrupulous magic user stumbling upon them by accident."

Wash snorted with laughter, and AJ was momentarily mesmerized by the pure joy radiating from him. "I just pictured some bearded guy in a ceremonial robe, standing next to an inscribed pentagram and waving his arms while he tried to summon Stanley. Or Fred. Or, gods forbid, Ashley."

Without thinking, AJ shifted his vision to the astral, and, despite the bespelled glasses, Wash's *calon* nearly blinded him with its glory. "Are you certain about your limited power?"

"Familiars are never wrong. If none of 'em wanted me, then they didn't see me as witch material." He glanced at his watch. "Whoops. We'd better haul ass. You don't want to be late. What's your first class?"

Suddenly AJ lost all desire for his tea. "Patient Assessment and Diagnostics."

Wash grimaced. "That's Dr. Mori's class."

"Is that bad? Should I be worried?"

"Oh, she's great, don't get me wrong. But she can be pretty intimidating."

AJ's belly plummeted to his feet in their odd canvas shoes. "She's not a magician, is she? Or... or a necromancer?"

"Necromancer? In a hospital? Not likely. Nope, she's a kitsune. She just earned her eighth tail, so she's not somebody you want to mess with, but she's damn good at what she does. Come on. I'll show you the classroom."

Although Wash kept up a steady commentary, pointing out hospital features as he led AJ through the corridors, AJ barely registered the words. Of all the things he'd been in his life—and there were many, if he included the professions of all the humans he'd possessed—he'd never been a simple student, answerable to nobody but himself and his instructors. *I'm not sure I know how to begin.*

He glanced at Wash and allowed his vision to shift to the astral so he could bask in that glow again. He swore he could feel its warmth encompassing him, cocooning him, reassuring him that he wasn't alone.

They stopped outside a door marked *Classroom A*. Wash patted AJ on the shoulder. "Here you go. Good luck."

AJ nearly grabbed Wash's hand and begged him to enter the room with him, but Wash had his own duties. AJ shouldn't impose any further. "Thank you. For everything."

"Don't mention it." He raised a hand in farewell and strode off down the hall as if he knew exactly where he was going.

I wish I knew where I was going. His immediate destination, however, was this room. He took a deep breath and slipped inside. The cluster of orbs at the front of the room startled him until he realized he hadn't shifted back to mundane vision. But before he did, he checked out the signature of each *calon*.

Witch. Witch. Fae. Shifter. Witch. Shifter. Were.

Good. At least there were no magicians.

He crept along the wall and, leaving an empty row between him and the others, seated himself on the aisle. One of the students—the fae—smiled tentatively, but most simply ignored him, their attention absorbed by the screens of their cell phones.

A door at the front of the classroom opened and a woman strode in. She had a smooth cap of blue-black hair and was wearing a white lab coat over a severe blouse and straight gray trousers. "Good morning." Her sharp gaze caught AJ's. "You must be the new student from the Sheol Retraining Initiative. How shall we call you?"

AJ breathed a sigh of relief. At least the doctor knew better than to ask for his name. Perhaps this wouldn't be so bad. "AJ, if you please, magistra."

Her lips twitched. "As I'm not a witch, the correct form of address is doctor." She strode to a podium equipped with a keyboard and monitor. "Please turn to page 247 in *Medical Diagnostics: Mundane and Arcane*."

The other students pulled out their books and cracked them open at once. Apparently Dr. Mori expected instant obedience. AJ folded his hands and awaited her next instruction.

Instead, she said "AJ," in a tone that could freeze Sheol's lava river. "Why haven't you opened your book as I requested?"

He blinked. "I don't have it with me."

Her lips thinned. "I understand that demons thrive on chaos, but in this program, we cannot tolerate rebellion or lack of discipline. Lives may depend upon it."

"Of course, magis— Doctor."

"Yet you have already put a foot wrong by attending my class unprepared. I objected strongly to admitting a student in the middle of the term, but I was overruled."

All the other students swiveled in their seats to stare at him. He couldn't tell whether they were sympathetic or simply relieved that they weren't the focus of the doctor's irritation.

AJ had never wished so desperately that he could sink through the floor. Unfortunately, he couldn't go completely astral without a subject to possess. "I'm sorry, doctor. If you wish me to carry the book, I can retrieve it now."

"No. I don't wish to disrupt the class any further, and I never tolerate late entry. Please leave. For tomorrow's class, see that you come prepared."

"Yes, doctor."

AJ slunk out of the room, closing the door softly behind him, then leaned against it, trying to calm his jittering nerves.

An eternity in Sheol was looking better every minute.

Chapter Three

Since the frost giant still hadn't fully recovered, poor guy, life in the large-being ward was still rather, er, lively. The second time Wash returned from delivering a cart full of soiled linens to the basement laundry, calculating how long it would be before his *next* trip, he nearly missed the figure cowering on the bench overlooking the courtyard.

"AJ?" Wash hurried over. "What are you doing here? Was class dismissed early?"

AJ shook his head, shoulders drooping. "She kicked me out."

Wash frowned as he hunkered down next to AJ's knees. "What for?"

"I didn't bring my textbook."

"Wow. That's really random. I know she can be strict, but I'd think she'd cut you a little slack on your first day."

"Apparently she objects to my being here. She considers demons chaotic and disruptive." His full lips twisted in a wry smile. "I can't honestly say that she's wrong."

"Bullshit. She doesn't know you yet, so she had no excuse to be so harsh. Although if you don't mind my asking, why *didn't* you bring the book? Did you forget?"

"I didn't realize having the tome in hand was so important."

"I think it's more that she wants you to reference parts of the book during the lecture."

"But the book's physical presence isn't necessary for that."

Wash chuckled. "Right. The only way that'd be true is if you had the whole thing memorized."

AJ's eyes behind the glint of the spectacle spell were so freaking sad. "That's right."

"What do you mean, 'That's right'?"

"I have the book memorized. I didn't realize that carrying it was required for class attendance." He frowned, shaking his head. "Stupid of me. I've had experience with the ceremonial properties of key artifacts. I simply didn't realize the book was ritually significant."

"Hold on a sec. You have *Medical Diagnostics: Mundane and Arcane* memorized? All of it?"

AJ's eyebrows quirked up as if Wash were asking ridiculous questions. "Yes."

"But that thing's gotta weigh six pounds."

"Six point two. Two of the others were larger, but the last four were only three pounds or so."

Wash dropped down onto his butt. "'Were'? You can't have memorized them too."

Again with that perplexed head tilt. "Why not?"

"Seven textbooks? You memorized seven textbooks in one night?"

"Not quite. I spent some of the time on the..." AJ's gaze skittered away, and he bit his lip. "The *other* books. The... the kissing books."

Kissing books? Oh. Wash chuckled. "I'm guessing the last person who lived in that room left some romance novels behind."

AJ nodded. "They were *wonderful*. I never knew—"

"Let's go back to the main issue here." Wash stood up and extended a hand to pull AJ off the bench. "How fast do you read?"

AJ shrugged. "The passage of chronological time isn't relevant. If I have knowledge to consume, whether printed or"—he swallowed convulsively, his throat working as if he were fighting nausea—"or *otherwise*, I'm able to do so in the allotted interval."

"So super speed reading? Wow. Really?"

"Yes. Although it wouldn't be very useful without the perfect recall, of course."

"In other words, you don't have to carry your textbook with you in order to have the material at your fingertips. Or…" He flicked his fingers at AJ's head. "Wherever." AJ nodded. "Can all demons do that?"

"No. Our abilities vary based on our purpose. I was manifested as a library assistant for Samigina, a marquis of Sheol who teaches liberal sciences. The ability to absorb information, transcribe or translate if necessary, and locate it at my progenitor's command was one of my basic protocols."

Wash raised his eyebrows. "Sheol has libraries?"

"Perhaps not the kind you imagine. Only in the sense that high-level demons, depending on their proclivities, may collect books, the rarer the better. They aren't inclined to *lend* the books, you understand. For them, *owning* them is the goal."

"Okay, putting all that aside for now—and I really want to hear more about it sometime, because Sheol sounds *crazy*—why didn't you tell Dr. Mori that before she tossed you out on your ear?"

AJ blinked. "She demanded the presence of the book, not a recital of its contents."

"I think we need to have a little talk about the difference between the spirit and the letter of the law. Come on."

Wash took AJ's elbow and hauled him down the corridor.

"Where are we going?"

"Back to class."

AJ jerked out of Wash's hold. "I... I can't. She told me not to come back until tomorrow. With the book."

Wash tapped AJ's forehead. "You've got the book, dude. You just need to tell her."

AJ's eyes grew as round as a sylph's, and he backed away. "Contradict someone in authority? I couldn't. I never have. It's... it's just not *done*."

"Maybe not in Sheol or in some douche bag magician's laboratory. But you're not in those shitholes anymore. Sure, you should show respect to people who've earned it by their training or ability or character, but you're allowed to stand up for yourself. Hells, in this business, it's critical for you to express your opinion or offer pertinent information—like, for instance, that you're the freaking walking Wikipedia—especially when it affects patient care or your own well-being."

"But... but..."

AJ looked so terrified that Wash wanted nothing more than to wrap him in a hug, but he settled for gripping AJ's shoulders and looking him square in the eyes. "What you can do is pretty remarkable. In fact, I don't know of anybody else in any realm who can do the same, so it's not a surprise that Dr. Mori wouldn't expect it. But she's not an asshole, you know? She's just no-nonsense, which is kinda counterintuitive for a kitsune. When you think about it, they're agents of chaos, too, same as demons. But when everyone assumes you're out to incite mayhem, it's easy to veer so far in the other direction that you look like you've got a rune stick up your ass."

AJ winced. "I understand that's a figure of speech, but during the Inquisition, it was more descriptive than I care to remember."

"Trigger warning. Got it. I guess I'd better watch my use of colorful metaphors."

"I'm sorry. I have some issues with being too literal. It's an artifact of being bound. I had to do precisely what my master instructed—"

It was Wash's turn to wince. "I wish you wouldn't say that."

AJ blinked. "Instructed?"

"No. 'Master.' I don't like to think about you being enslaved."

AJ smiled sadly. "Neither do I. But since more demons will be arriving here in the Upper World in the not too distant future, it's best if everyone understands how we function. Those who bargain for souls craft contracts that are as advantageous as possible for them. Frequently it's a turn of phrase or interpretation of a particular word that means the difference between damnation and freedom. For those of us who have been bound, we seek the loophole in any instruction given us, any way for us to escape. An instant of rebellion to remind us that we have wills of our own, no matter how our masters—in Sheol or the Upper World—may wish it were otherwise."

Something twisted in Wash's middle. How many years —how many centuries—had AJ been searching for a way out? "*This* is your life now. A new chance. How about starting out with a little empowerment?"

"Empowerment?"

"Yup. By proving why you deserve to be in that class."

AJ stared at the classroom door, Wash's presence the only thing that kept him from bolting back to his room. "Are you sure? She gave me a direct command."

"She's your teacher. Not your master. Someday she might be your boss, but remember, you're not bound by anything other than hospital regulations, common decency, and your own character now. Got it?"

AJ nodded, but he still couldn't make himself open the door. "Would you—" He gulped. Could he do this? He'd never been allowed to ask for anything before. Not something for himself alone. *A new world. A new life. Empowerment.* Although begging for someone to hold his hand wasn't exactly powerful. *I don't care.* "W-w-would you come with me? Even though she said not to disrupt the class again?"

Wash smiled and placed a hand on AJ's shoulder. "Sure." His grin widened. "They're kind of used to me disrupting things around here. Let's go."

AJ nodded, and, buoyed by Wash's touch, opened the door and stepped inside.

He almost turned and ran, because Dr. Mori stopped mid-sentence and stared stonily at him while every student swiveled in their seat, their faces awash in astonishment, apprehension, or in at least one case, anticipation.

Wash waved cheerfully. "Hey, Doc."

"Mr. Hernández. I don't recall requesting your presence."

"Nope. But you know how I hate it when natural consequences are in direct opposition to what's best for the hospital."

"I presume you believe now to be one of those times."

"Yup." He turned to AJ and placed a gentle hand on his back, just below his wing slits. "Go ahead. Tell her."

Tell her what? Tell her how? AJ shifted from foot to foot, his instincts screaming at him to hedge or hide. Instead, with Wash's touch to bolster him, he took a deep breath. *When in doubt, example speaks louder than explanation.* "'If the blood host takes warfarin, the vampire may experience anaphylaxis similar to ingesting shifter blood, although in a much milder form.'"

Dr. Mori's eyes narrowed, her face taking on a distinctly foxy cast. And were those tails sprouting from under her lab coat? "How is this pertinent to the interruption?"

"It's, um, the first sentence on page 247 of *Medical Diagnostics: Mundane and Arcane.*"

She blinked, her tails twitching, as several of the students rifled through the pages in the books.

"He's right," the fae in the front row murmured.

Dr. Mori glared them into silence. "Would you care to explain yourself, AJ?"

AJ fought the urge to retreat. "I have perfect recall. Since I read all the textbooks last night, I can—"

"Wait." Her eyes blazed gold. "You read *all* the books? Last night?"

He nodded. "I read very, um, rapidly."

"I see," she said slowly, tapping one nail on the podium. "O'Rourke. Page 73, paragraph two, third sentence."

Is giving me the author instead of the book title another test? Not that it mattered. When AJ read a book, he read and remembered *everything*, even the copyright notice. "'In the case of a displaced fracture, the bones must be realigned, which may require surgery.'"

She glanced at the fae student again, who nodded. "Rhys-Jones. Page 484. Paragraph one, second sentence."

This time, all the students fumbled with their texts, but AJ didn't wait for them. "'Severe eczema in dryads may resemble tree bark.'"

"Gowdie. Page 327. Paragraph one." AJ folded his hands in front of him and remained silent. "Well?"

He shrugged apologetically. "That book only has three hundred and twenty-two pages. There's nothing to recite."

One of the students snickered, and Wash grinned, wide and beautiful. *Approval.* AJ had never experienced such a thing and wished he could bask in it for hours. Whenever he'd completed a task for one of his mage masters, they were more likely to complain because he hadn't been quick enough, or because the results weren't what they'd hoped. He'd never been certain how they expected him to make a poor man richer so they could extract more money from him or make an ignorant man suddenly aware of the information they sought.

This time, he'd accomplished something for *himself.* Granted, he'd had to be prodded, but the result was the same. And somebody was *happy* about it.

Unfortunately, the doctor wasn't that person.

She gripped the edges of the podium. "Regurgitating words does not constitute comprehension or analysis."

"I understand, doctor. I only wished to demonstrate why I didn't bring my books with me. Or rather why toting the physical books isn't necessary." He tapped his forehead. "I carry them up here."

"I see." Her eyes lost some of their glow. "In that case, I owe you an apology, although I'm uncertain why you didn't explain yourself in the first place."

At the doctor's tart tone, AJ dropped his gaze to his feet, hunching his shoulders in the position he had always assumed when one of the masters accused him of insubordination. The doctor cursed under her breath. "Sheol. Of course. You've never confronted an authority figure before, have you?"

Wash rubbed circles on AJ's back, a sunburst of warmth that emboldened AJ to raise his chin and meet the doctor's gaze. "No, doctor. The master was always right."

Her mouth quirked up. "Even when they were completely wrong, I take it."

Since the doctor was no longer glaring at him, and since Wash's touch was lending AJ courage, he straightened his shoulders. "Although I do have a question."

AJ paused, waiting for her to grant him permission, but Wash elbowed him in the ribs. "Go ahead and ask."

"On page 196, Gowdie references a particular treatment for pneumonia that's in direct opposition to what Chang says on page 263. But neither of those authors take into account the differences in the *calon* between supernatural species. They both assume a human patient."

The doctor's features were now decidedly foxy, and there were at least three tails in evidence beneath her coat.

Her pants must have special properties. "That's true. Humans are the physiological baseline. Bone, muscle, internal organs. Most are the same or similar, regardless of species."

"But not always. Demons, being purpose-built, rarely conform to the human norm, but since we're fairly indestructible and not subject to systemic illnesses, I suppose it wouldn't make sense to include us in any general medical texts. However, the internal differences in other species aren't always trivial despite outward appearance. In 1527, Paracelsus said that if you attempt —"

"Wait." The doctor's tone was sharp, eroding AJ's confidence again. "You know Paracelsus's *Treatise on Fantastic Creatures*?"

Would they send him away for something like that? When his master at the time had procured a copy, it was illegal. In fact, he'd been burned at the stake for it. "Of course."

"The whole treatise? Not just the fragments?"

"Yes. The codex as well."

"But it's been lost for centuries."

AJ tapped his forehead. "Not entirely."

Wash whooped, earning a severe glare from the doctor. "AJ, I want to speak to you during my office hours about transcribing the text. I'd like you to provide a bibliography of all the books in your memory as well."

AJ glanced sidelong at Wash, heat washing up his throat. "All of them?"

"All of them that pertain to medicine and health-related subjects. The others"—she lifted an eyebrow—"you may keep private."

"Yes, doctor."

"In the meantime, I'm transferring you to the clinical practicum track. I see no point in making you sit through lectures on material you've already mastered. I believe Mr. Hernández can escort you to the class, which is already in session." She glared at the other students. "As, I remind you, is this one. You lot get ready to tell me the reasons Gowdie and Chang might disagree on their approach to lower respiratory ailments, and why either of those treatments might be contraindicated for selkies in particular. AJ, you are excused."

Chapter Four

Once outside in the corridor, Wash let out another whoop and did a little victory dance. AJ, poor guy, looked bewildered as all get-out.

"What just happened?"

"You tested out of a year's worth of classes, that's what. Now come on." Wash grabbed AJ's arm and towed him down the hall. "My brother's in charge of the practicum track. You'll love him. He's great." He grinned. "Although not nearly as handsome as me."

AJ regarded him solemnly. "Nobody could be."

Wash's steps faltered. He'd had his share of hookups, even had a steady boyfriend for a couple of years. When it came down to a permanent commitment, though, nobody wanted to tie themselves to a defective witch.

But AJ's sincere, matter-of-fact pronouncement made him want to strut like a Sidhe lord. Why did it mean so much more? *Maybe because I know he's got baggage too.* Although unlike Wash, he certainly didn't lack for skills.

"Thanks. But I was just being an ass. I didn't mean it."

"I did. Your *calon* is brighter than a Beltane bonfire."

Wash patted AJ's back. "Maybe we should get the spell checked on your specs, buddy, because that's crazy talk. You don't have to try to make me feel better."

"I'm not." AJ shrugged. "I speak the literal truth. Because, you know, literal is all I've ever known."

"Yeah, well, we'll work on that. Otherwise how will you ever manage to blow off an annoying assignment by convincing your instructor that a hippogriff ate your homework?"

AJ drew himself up, red flickering in the depths of his eyes. "I would never—"

"This is it." Wash grasped the door handle of Operating Theater 2, although he didn't release his hold on AJ. For some reason, that just seemed wrong. "It's not as formal as Dr. Mori's lectures, so don't be nervous. Ready?"

"Will you come in with me?"

Wash glanced down at his fingers on AJ's bare skin. *They look perfect there.* "Do you want me to?"

AJ touched the back of Wash's hand. "Please."

At that touch, that plea, Wash's eyes prickled. Sure, he was the go-to guy for bedpan patrol and wrangling oversized patients, but other than Ky, nobody had ever wanted him just for comfort and reassurance. "I'd be honored."

So they walked into the room together.

A half-dozen students were gathered in the center of the room along with Ky and his work partner, Pete. They were all looking at the occupant of a plus-sized gurney.

"Geez," Wash murmured, "I always forget how big trows are."

AJ edged closer to Wash and murmured, "I thought trows were all short."

"Depends on the bloodline. Some of 'em can give frost giants a run for their kroner."

Ky glanced up and smiled. "Wash. You're just in time. You can help move this big guy to the treatment table."

"Trust you to put me to work." Wash released AJ—*still feels wrong*—and approached the group, AJ close behind him. *Goddess bless, do all demons run so hot?* Scrubs weren't great at masking body heat, and AJ's was scorching. "But I'm here to deliver a new student to you. This is AJ. Dr. Mori just assigned him to this track, and I told him he'd like you, so don't be a douche bag."

Ky rolled his eyes. "And this, class, is what happens when you work with your brother. No respect." But he gestured for AJ to join the rest of the group. "Welcome to class, AJ. You're part of the Sheol Retraining Initiative, right?"

AJ edged closer to Wash. "Yes. Is that a problem?"

"Not a bit. I was hoping we'd get at least one demon here at St. Stupid's. As I understand it, demons are adept at evaluating a subject's needs. Am I right?"

AJ gulped, moving even closer. Wash could feel him trembling. "It's okay. Remember what I told you? Expressing your opinion is important."

AJ jerked his chin down once, then his shoulders rose with a huge breath. "No, that's not precisely correct." As soon as the words were out of his mouth, he seemed to fold in on himself. "I beg your pardon."

Okay, confidence-building is gonna take some time, I guess.

From her perch in the corner, Ky's African grey parrot familiar, Zuri, muttered, "Stupid."

AJ flinched, but Ky just chuckled. "Don't mind Zuri. She's talking to me, not you. I've always thought that having someone who could tell us what a patient needs independently would be great for triage and diagnostic medicine. After all, many times they can't describe what's wrong, and even if they're able to speak, they may not be forthcoming."

Wash leaned over and mock-whispered in AJ's ear. "In other words, they lie."

Ky gave Wash the stink-eye, but his voice was perfectly level when he said, "Or they might be intimidated by the environment, or by someone *in* the environment." He glanced at AJ, understanding flickering in his dark eyes.

"Demons..." AJ's voice was rough, and he cleared his throat. "Demons can perceive *desires*. However, what someone *wants* is not always what that person *needs*. For evaluating needs, you'd be better off with a djinn."

Ky chuckled. "That'd be a coup, wouldn't it? But no djinn has been sighted since the fall of Persia. Still, knowing what somebody wants might give us important information as well." He gestured to the trow. "For instance, our patient here hasn't regained consciousness since Pete and I picked it up at the foot of Watson Falls. We don't know why it was there, since trows aren't normally allowed to leave Faerie, or how it managed to break its femur, since trow bones are about as fragile as granite. Knowing what it wants might give us a place to start. Wash, if you could help shift it now, so we're ready when the doctor arrives?"

As Wash circled to the head of the gurney, AJ peered at the trow, his brow knotted. "It wants to punch you in the face."

"I thought... demons... could only... on three, guys," Ky said as they worked the backboard under the trow. "Read conscious people. One... two..."

"It *is* conscious."

The trow's eyes popped open, red and wild. Its hand shot up, and with a roar, it wrapped one giant hand around Wash's throat.

With his arm trapped under the backboard, Wash could only curse silently as the trow's grip tightened.

He gasped vainly for air, dots sparking and dancing before his eyes. Chaos erupted around him as students scattered, Zuri circling overhead. Ky jammed a needle into the trow's arm, only to have it snap against the rock-hard muscle. As his vision started to tunnel, Wash met AJ's horrified gaze. Oxygen deprivation must be giving him hallucinations, because as everything faded to black, he could swear AJ had eight arms.

AJ didn't hesitate, didn't think, didn't *breathe*. Instinct took over, and his wings ripped through the back of his shirt as his six astral arms solidified, tearing through the side seams. He launched himself forward and up, scattering the other students, ignoring the squawking bird that flapped overhead, discounting the shouts of Ky and Pete, and hovered over the gods-bedamned trow who *dared* put its hands on Wash.

With the strength bred into him by his progenitor, he slapped the trow down, pinning it to the gurney with three hands while another three pried the bastard's fingers from Wash's neck. Pete caught Wash and hustled him away. Dimly, AJ was aware of Ky approaching with a giant syringe, but with Wash out of reach, he was focused on the trow. The glare from AJ's eyes spilled over, bathing the trow's snarling face in red.

"Keep. Your hands. To *yourself*," he growled.

Ky inserted the needle into the trow's massive arm, and its struggles gradually ceased, its inner eyelids flickering to half-mast, but AJ didn't release his hold. *Not yet. Not until I know Wash is safe.*

The trow's thoughts grew disjointed and then vanished into murky semi-consciousness, but still AJ held on.

"AJ." Ky's voice was gentle. "The patient's out. You can let go now." AJ didn't. Who knew when the medication would wear off and put Wash in danger again? Ky huffed. "Wash?"

Then Wash's hand was on AJ's back, smoothing the skin below his wings. "It's okay, big guy. I'm okay. You were awesome, but you can stand down now."

AJ blinked, then glanced around. Ky and Pete stood near the trow's head. Pete was checking the pulse in its neck, but Ky was focused on AJ. The other students cowered against the wall or behind equipment, their terror nearly visible in the air. *I've frightened them. I never wanted to frighten anyone again.*

AJ let go and dropped to his knees next to the gurney, hunching over as he furled his wings and dematerialized his arms. "I'm sorry. I didn't mean to scare anyone."

Wash knelt next to him, his hand warm on AJ's bare shoulder. "Hey. Don't apologize." AJ glanced up at the scratchiness in Wash's voice. "You didn't scare anyone. Well, other than the trow, but I'm cool with that."

"But look at them," AJ whispered, jerking his head toward the other students, who were now gathered around an earnestly speaking Ky. "They were terrified."

"They were terrified by an out-of-control trow. If you hadn't stopped it…" Wash's hand tightened on AJ's shoulder. "Well, let's say Ky is pretty damn fast with a syringe, but I don't think even he could have prevented someone from being seriously injured.

"But you." AJ sat back on his heels, searching Wash's face, chest tightening at the livid marks on Wash's neck. "Your voice. Your— It could have killed you."

"But it didn't. Because of you." Wash's smile lit AJ up from inside. "And holy crap, AJ. Where the hells do you keep eight freaking arms?"

"Oh. They're in the astral. I can manifest them when needed, since they were useful for carrying stacks of books." He shrugged diffidently. "My progenitor thought it a great joke to give me a name that means 'octopus.' Of course, his inability to keep the joke to himself may be one of the reasons that my first magician master was able to discover my name and bind me."

Wash's gaze darkened. "Well, nobody's gonna learn anything you don't want them to know. Not anymore. Not from us." He teetered a bit, his legs obviously still shaky, so AJ leaped up to wrap an arm around his waist. "Yo, Ky? This incident stays on the down-low, yeah?"

Ky glanced over, and although his eyes narrowed as his gaze flicked from Wash to AJ, he nodded and turned back to the other students. "Patient treatment of any kind is covered under the hospital's confidentiality regulations. Am I clear?" The students nodded reluctantly. "If any video of AJ's *completely reasonable response* should find its way onto the web, there will be consequences." He stared at one witch who had a cell phone clutched in her hand. "I don't need to remind you of the severity of those consequences, do I?"

She gulped, shaking her head wildly as she punched at the screen.

"See? All sorted." Wash plucked a shred of ruined scrubs off AJ's belly. "How about we get you another shirt?"

"But... But you were attacked." AJ raised his fingers but didn't go so far as to touch Wash's neck, where the imprint of the trow's hand was already starting to bruise. "This is a hospital. Surely you should be receiving treatment."

"I already did. I'm fine." His voice turned hoarse on the last word and he cleared his throat. "Although I could use something to drink." He smiled at AJ. "Come to the cafeteria with me?"

"Of course. Unless..." His shoulders hunched again. "My actions must have consequences as well. Do I need to submit myself for punishment?"

"What? No!"

Ky appeared at Wash's shoulder. "Not punishment. Although I would like to chat with you about your abilities."

AJ hung his head. "Of course. I'm sorry."

"No apologies." Ky grinned at him. "That was a truly awesome demonstration. But here at St. Stupid's, we're not above exploiting our staff's capabilities. Right now, we have to transport this joker"—he jerked his head at the unconscious trow—"to the OR. Class will reconvene after lunch." Ky clapped AJ on the shoulder. "Good job. Wash can be an irritating cuss, but I'd like to keep him around. So thank you."

He and Pete wheeled the trow out a set of double doors as AJ stared after them, jaw slack.

Wash peered at him. "Is something wrong?"

"He... He *thanked* me. Nobody has ever thanked me before." AJ blinked. "Nobody has ever complimented my performance before either."

Wash muttered something under his breath, then squared his shoulders. "Well, get used to it. Because something tells me you're going to hear it a lot. Now, how about that drink?"

Chapter Five

Wash held the supply room door for AJ. "So." *Damn, I should have hit Ky up for a hyssop lozenge so I don't sound like a three-sage-smudge-a-day hack.* He cleared his throat and fought a wince. *Yikes. Bad idea.* "You've got wings, six extra arms you keep tucked away in some other dimension, and you can read faster than the wind. Hiding any other mad skills?"

AJ huddled against a rack of shelves full of ritual candles, crystals, and prepackaged herbs, his arms—one set only—folded over his truly magnificent chest. His smooth brown skin glowed under the fluorescent overhead lights. *I wonder if all demons have hairless chests?*

"Perfect recall. Don't forget that." AJ shuddered. "I never can."

"Shit," Wash muttered. *Don't perv on the half-naked demon when he's suffering a post-traumatic event reaction.* Wash held out his hands, an invitation for AJ to clasp them—which, thank the stars, he did. "You're not gonna relive that, are you? Let it weigh on you? Because you did great."

AJ sighed, his gaze focused on their joined hands. "I can file it away. At least my progenitor gave me *that*, although he probably intended it as an efficiency aid rather than a kindness. But the memory will always be there. The trow's hand closing around your throat." His grip tightened. "The absolute knowledge that its greatest desire was to watch the life drain from your eyes, even if... Even if..."

"Even if what?" Wash murmured.

"Even if it was so crazed with pain that it was barely rational." AJ lifted his gaze to Wash's, his expression bleak. "I didn't *care*, Wash. Not about its reasons or its feelings. I would have killed it with no regret to save you. That's not the response of a medical professional. That's the response of—"

"Of somebody who cares. Come here." Wash gathered AJ into his arms, caressing the soft skin on his back, the ridges that concealed his wings, the hidden pearls of his spine. "First, you're not trained. Hells, you haven't gotten through a single class yet."

AJ snorted against Wash's shoulder, a ridiculously adorable sound. "So not only am I a physical danger to others, I'm ignorant. Dr. Mori was right. I'm chaotic and disruptive."

"Nonsense." Wash stroked AJ's hair, the curls springy under his palm. "It was an instinctive response, and you were the only person there with the chops to pull it off."

"But the thing is..." AJ sighed. When he pulled away, Wash felt oddly bereft. "I don't think I would have had the same reaction with anybody else. I reacted because *you* were the one in danger. I couldn't let the trow hurt *you*."

Heat infused Wash's chest. "Yeah?"

AJ nodded. "Remember I told you that the textbooks weren't the only books I read last night?"

"Uh-huh."

"There were things in those other books. Things I've never dreamed of." AJ's eyes morphed from inky dark to molten gold. "Things I want to try. With you."

"What—" Wash's voice nearly vanished, and he had to clear his throat again. *Screw the pain.* "What kind of things?"

"Things like this." AJ leaned forward slowly, slowly, slowly, and Wash could barely breathe. Then their lips were touching and *merciful goddess.*

The kiss wasn't practiced—how could it be, when it was AJ's first? But even slightly off-target, it still sent heat sizzling along Wash's veins to pool under his heart until his chest felt three times its normal size.

Wash stifled a groan, but AJ must have sensed it because he jerked back, covering his mouth with both hands.

"I'm sorry." The glow in his eyes snuffed out. "Beelzebub's horns, I'm so sorry."

Wash had to blink for a moment, shaking his head to bring his brain back online. "Why?"

"I didn't *ask*. All those books. They said consent was critical. And nobody should know that better than I do."

Ah, goddess. The poor guy. When was the last time anyone asked for his consent? "It's okay." But AJ just shook his head, backing away, tremors chasing across the skin of his bare chest. "In fact, if you don't mind, I'd like to kiss you again."

AJ froze like a familiar in the headlights. "You... you do?"

"Yes. Because I've got to tell you... I mean, I'm not a virgin, but I've never had a kiss that lit me up like that one."

AJ blinked, his pretty eyes kindling again. "Really?" His gaze drifted to Wash's chest and his lips formed an O. "Your *calon*. I didn't think it could get any brighter, but—"

"Never mind that." Wash held out a hand. "Come back? The first kiss was incredible, but I think we can get even better with a little practice."

A slow smile curved AJ's lips, and he took Wash's hand, allowing Wash to draw him in until they were chest to chest. Wash mentally cursed his stupid scrub shirt, because what would it be like to be skin to skin?

Wash cradled AJ's face in his hands. "Are all demons this smooth? Or has Sheol cornered the market on really close shaves?"

"I don't have a beard." AJ's voice was faint, nearly breathless. "My progenitor thought caring for it would interfere with the time spent on more important tasks."

"Let me guess. *His* tasks, right?"

"Yes. It's one of the only things I was ever grateful to him for. Until today."

Wash ran a finger along the curve of AJ's top lip, eliciting a shiver. "What about today?"

AJ captured Wash's hand and pressed a kiss to his palm, sending another *zing* along Wash's nerves. "Without my wings and my additional arms, I might not have been able to save you."

This time, Wash didn't bother to stifle his groan. He angled his head and dove in for another kiss. AJ's mouth was even softer than his cheeks. *Addictive.* Wash flicked his tongue along the plump bottom lip and when AJ gasped, he delved deeper. *He tastes like burnt sugar. So freaking delicious.*

AJ pulled back, trembling, and leaned his forehead against Wash's. "Is that... The books mentioned that tongues could be involved, but I never realized it could feel like *that*."

A frisson of unease skated down Wash's spine. "Was it okay? I mean, not everybody likes that kind of kiss, which is perfectly fine, but—"

"I liked it. I *loved* it. I love how we... we *fit*."

Wash grinned. "Yeah, we do, don't we? You're exactly the right height for me."

"I am?"

"Yep. We line up. Shoulder to shoulder." Wash flexed his pecs, his nipples brushing AJ's. "Chest to..." *Wait a minute. Where'd my shirt go?*

"You make me feel things I've never felt before. Sensations that... Well, I've *read* about them..." AJ glanced down, where his scrub pants were distended by a very impressive erection. His eyebrows bunched together as he studied Wash's groin. "You don't seem to have the same problem.

Wash's chuckle was a bit strained because of how binding his underwear was. Since the supply closet didn't run to tighty-whities, poor AJ didn't even have that much armor. *Maybe we both need to invest in some steel-reinforced briefs if we're gonna run into each other in the hospital corridors.* "Trust me. I feel something all right." Wash tucked AJ's hand against his chest and leaned in for another kiss. "Fire."

Next to them, the wick on a ritual black candle burst into flame.

"Shit!" Wash let go of AJ and pinched the wick, snuffing out the fire, then shook his fingers, continuing to curse under his breath

He's hurt. AJ grabbed Wash's hand, studying the tips of his fingers. They weren't blistered, not even reddened, but sometimes that happened later. "Do you need treatment? Burn ointment? Pain relievers?"

Wash flipped his hand and laced their fingers together. "I'm fine. Didn't even feel the heat." But he frowned, staring at the thread of smoke rising from the charred wick. "But that shouldn't have happened. Ritual candles can't spontaneously combust. You can't even light them with an ordinary match. It takes an active witch—either a female or a male with a familiar bond—to call the fire."

To AJ, the candle flame had barely registered, overshadowed as it was by the sheer brilliance of Wash's *calon. My vision. I never switched from the astral.* But another glow caught his eye, and he glanced down. A red-gold cord led from beneath AJ's heart to the same spot on Wash's chest.

AJ sucked in a breath and backed up until he slammed against more shelves, their metal edges cold and rough on his bare shoulders. He shut down his astral vision so he couldn't see the evidence of his breach of Wash's trust.

Wash peered at him, concern knotting his forehead. "AJ? What's wrong?"

AJ tried to speak, but nothing came out. He gestured from his chest to Wash's, which, now that the glow of his *calon* was extinguished, was as bare as AJ's own.

Wash glanced down. "Yeah. I know. Weird, huh? Is that another demon thing? Clothing dematerialization? Useful, that. I was just wishing that my shirt wasn't in the way of feeling your skin on mine, but—"

"You wished for it?" AJ croaked. "For your shirt to vanish?"

"Yeah." Wash drew the word out. "So?"

"So you willed your shirt to vanish. And then you called fire."

Wash frowned. "It couldn't have been me. My *calon* is malformed. I don't have a familiar and never will. This has gotta be you."

"I can't call fire. I'm explicitly incapable of it because fire would have been a danger to my progenitor's books." AJ let his vision veer into the astral and there it was again —the undeniable link, the footprint of a possession, although he'd never seen one this color before. Usually they were more virulent: fire-shot purple or poisonous chartreuse. "And as for clothes, the fact that I destroyed my shirt when I unfurled my wings and manifested my arms proves how unprepared I am for even *wearing* them, let alone managing their appearance or disappearance."

Wash raised a shaking hand to his mouth. "What are you saying?" His voice was barely audible over the pounding of AJ's heart.

"I think... I'm afraid I've possessed you. Sort of."

Wash's eyebrows shot up. "Possessed me? But I don't feel any different."

"I don't understand it either, but there's a tether." He gestured between his chest and Wash's. "I can see it. Although I haven't possessed you fully, we at least have a link. A connection." AJ pushed against the panic that threatened to close his throat. "A conduit for the exchange of power."

"What are you saying?"

AJ twitched with the need to touch Wash, to hold him. *And is that because I've tied us together, bound our fortunes and our lives?* "Don't you see? I'm built to be an assistant. That's why I was called into being. And isn't that what familiars do? Assist a witch? Become an intermediary, an *interface* for the magic you share with your triple goddess?"

Wash's golden-brown skin turned ashen. "You mean I'm *using* you? Like those bastard magicians? Like the demon overlords?"

"No! You haven't done anything wrong. I shared myself willingly." AJ offered a tentative smile. "Since no demon has ever been *asked* to share before, I had no idea that an astral link could form unbidden. We can't let it stand."

"Right." Something flickered across Wash's face. Sadness? Regret? AJ wished he were more adept at reading social cues. "You've only just gotten clear of unwanted chains. You wouldn't want another one."

"That's not it." He edged forward. "I know we've only just met, but if we didn't have an affinity, I don't think a spontaneous link could have been forged. However, whatever we're to become to one another, wouldn't you prefer it to be the result of choice, not chance?"

Wash scrubbed his hands over his face. "Goddess. The idea that I could actually *do* spellcraft." When he dropped his hands, his jaw tightened with determination. "You don't know how tempting it is for me to say *screw it* and let things stand. But if I take advantage of you to get what I want, I wouldn't be any better than those psychopathic magician assholes, and I don't even want to *think* what the natural consequences of that kind of selfishness would be."

AJ reached out, resting his fingers against Wash's shoulder. "Don't worry. You don't know my true name, so you can't enslave me."

Wash jerked out of reach. "Enslave you? I would never do that!" The truth of Wash's declaration vibrated along the tether and shivered in AJ's bones. Wash glanced down, touching his chest above his *calon*. "Did you feel that?"

AJ nodded. "You've made a vow with the ring of absolute truth. Now I know you won't ever victimize me. And I"—AJ placed his hand over his own *calon*—"will never do anything to hurt you."

Wash smiled, tapping his fingers against his bare skin. "Felt that too. Guess that means we can trust each other, huh?"

AJ nodded. "Yes. The vows will stand, even if the connection is severed, but I still think we would be better off if we forged it deliberately. Don't you?"

Wash shrugged. "Nobody knows why familiar bonds form, why familiars pick the witches they do. Since familiars don't speak, other than parrots like Zuri, and even she can't conduct a rational conversation, nobody ever will." He gestured between them, his fingers brushing the tether and making them both shiver. "Maybe we'll be able to shed some light on it."

"All the more reason to ask for help, don't you think?"

Wash sighed. "Yeah. I suppose. Damn you and your ethics." His grin robbed the words of any sting. "A demon with ethics. Who knew?"

"There are a lot of things about demons that the Upper World doesn't know." *Most of them for the best.*

"Right. Let's go talk to Dr. Mori."

"Why her?"

"She's head of diagnostic medicine." He gestured between them again. "And we need a diagnosis, right? But I don't think we should show up half-naked." He strode over to the shelves of folded scrubs and selected two shirts, then tossed one to AJ. "She only teaches in the morning, so maybe we can catch her in her office."

AJ struggled into his shirt, grateful that his nether regions had deflated enough to allow his pants to hang straight.

Wash paused by the door and reached out to stroke AJ's face. "But whatever happens, I'd definitely like to try kissing again. What do you say?"

AJ smiled, breath hitching. "I'd say brilliant."

"Excellent." Wash's answering grin lit up the room. "Now let's go get disconnected so we can get that particular party started."

Chapter Six

I called fire. I eliminated a barrier. Two of the basic spells all witches managed in their first months with a familiar. Wash was surprised he wasn't floating a foot off the floor as he and AJ hurried through the halls.

But his elation was tempered with guilt. He glanced at the gorgeous demon pacing solemnly by his side. *He says I'm not taking advantage of him, but how can I not? I get the ability to work spells, something I've wanted all my life. What does he get?*

Wash clenched his hands at his sides, his fingers fairly tingling with the urge to try something else before the ability was stripped away. But again, all the benefits were accruing to him. While Wash wouldn't object to the closeness required from a witch-familiar relationship—if that's really what this was—AJ had spent centuries being confined by the needs and demands of others. Maybe he'd want to enjoy his freedom a little more. Travel. Date other people, since he'd just discovered the joys of making out.

Wash's fists tightened until his nails bit into his palms. *I don't want him to make out with anyone else.* And not just because of the magical connection. AJ's lips, his taste, his touch—they ignited something in Wash he'd thought was as dormant as his magic. His gaze slid to AJ again. *Maybe he'll still want to date even if we're not magically attached at the hip.*

What if the connection couldn't be severed though? What if they'd somehow forged an unbreakable lifelong bond, like any witch and familiar? *I should feel guilty that I don't feel, well, more guilty about that possibility.*

They turned the last corner on the way to the elevators. Dr. Mori was standing in front of them, deep in serious conversation with Ky. As soon as Ky caught sight of Wash, he beckoned them over. Wash recognized the expression on Ky's face. He'd worn it the day he'd bonded with Zuri, the day Wash had failed for the third time to attract any familiar at the ceremony. *Remorse.*

Dr. Mori turned around. "Ah. AJ. You're just the person I wanted to see. Come with me."

Wash shared a glance with AJ, and Wash could swear he could hear the same worried thought flitting across AJ's mind—*How did she know?*

She strode down the hallway, but when Wash and AJ started to follow, Ky grasped Wash's arm. "You don't have to come. She just wants AJ."

AJ fumbled for Wash's hand, and Wash got the message. "I'm coming too. We need to talk to her, anyway."

"This might not be the best time—"

"Ky. Trust me on this one."

Ky heaved a sigh, the worried frown settling back on his face. "Okay then. On your head be it."

"That didn't sound ominous at all," Wash muttered. Hand-in-hand, he and AJ followed Ky into a patient room at the end of the hall where St. Stupid's joined the human wing of United Memorial.

The beep of equipment was as familiar to Wash as the sound of his own heartbeat, but his chest clenched at the sight of the small figure curled in a bed sized for much larger bodies.

Dr. Mori waited next to the EEG monitor. "AJ, as I understand it, you have extensive experience in human possession."

AJ's eyes widened, and he backed up a step. "I was bound at the time. I had no choice."

She waved his words away. "Yes, yes. That's understood." She grabbed a chart from its wall pocket and flipped through the pages. "We'd like you to possess this patient."

Jaw sagging, AJ shot a panicked glance at Wash. "You want me to *what*?"

She looked up, her brows bunched over her nose. "Are you having difficulty hearing? I understand that can happen in the transition from Sheol."

"No. I can hear you. But possession..." AJ started to shake. "I can't... You can't..." He backed all the way into the corner and sank down, hiding his face in his hands.

Wash glared at Dr. Mori. "Seriously, doctor? What the hells?"

She frowned at Wash as if he were a contaminant in her last Petrie dish. "Mr. Hernández, you're not required here."

"Really? Because I think I am. Clearly nobody else is concerned with AJ. For the triple goddess's sake, he was forced to possess people for centuries. You don't think that might be a trigger for him?"

She blinked. "He's been cleared for training by Dr. Kendrick."

"Yeah, for *medical* training. Not to get chucked right back into the same nightmare he's lived since the Middle Ages."

She sighed, setting the chart down on the bedside table. "One of the reasons we accepted him—"

"He's in the room, you know."

She faced AJ, who remained hidden behind his hands "I beg your pardon." She cleared her throat. "Let me be clear. The St. Stupid's administration didn't simply *accept* you into the training program. We *requested* you. Specifically."

When AJ didn't respond, Wash asked, "Why?"

"Because in the annals of demon summoning and possession, AJ is the only one who, when freed of restraint, didn't attempt to run amok."

AJ shook his head, still huddled in the corner. "I killed my last master."

"Exactly. That magician lost control of you. You could have remained in possession of his body, utilizing his skills and resources to establish a power base of your own. You chose instead to retreat into virtual exile in Sheol. You're the only demon we can trust with this case. Will you help us?"

Wash's presence, his hand resting between AJ's shoulder blades, penetrated the panic beating inside AJ's ribcage like a monster's heart.

"AJ. Are you okay?"

AJ shook his head. "No."

Wash chuckled. "Yeah. Sorry. Stupid question. Maybe I should ask what I can do to help?"

AJ peeked between his fingers. He and Wash were the only people in the room other than the tiny girl in the bed. "They've gone?"

"Just stepped outside for a minute." He settled down, legs crossed tailor-fashion, his shoulder pressed against AJ's. "Obviously they can't force you to do anything. You're not bound. You haven't completed your training. You have choices."

AJ glanced at the girl, immobile under the pale blue hospital blanket. Was she even breathing? "What's wrong with her?"

"They don't know. Ky brought her in to the human-side hospital, but the doctors there called in Dr. Mori. She's the head of diagnostic medicine for them too." He grinned crookedly. "Although of course they don't know that she's not as human as they are." He glanced at the bed. "The girl was taken out of a foster care situation, which of course put Ky on high alert, considering our background. She'd just gotten placed after being removed from her birth parents' home because of neglect."

AJ winced. "Abuse?"

Wash shook his head. "Her case worker said there didn't seem to be any sign of physical trauma, but she was uncommunicative. Her foster mom said she barely ate anything last night, her first with them, and this morning, she was completely catatonic."

"If she's unconscious, I can't possess her, anyway." For some reason, that saddened AJ. He never wanted to possess anybody again. Just the thought of it made panic carom around his chest again. But he would have liked to help this little girl, who sounded as if she'd had as little love and affection in her short life as AJ had had in his long one.

"She's not comatose. Just unresponsive. Turned in on herself."

"I've never possessed anybody voluntarily," AJ whispered, his gaze riveted on the girl's pale face. "My masters forced me in, holding onto the tether so they could pull me out before I could take advantage of the situation and try to escape." AJ snorted. "As if I could."

"So it's not a pleasant experience?"

"No!" He shivered, and Wash scooted closer, wrapping his arms around AJ's shoulders. "It's horrible. People hold on to their beliefs, their biases, their certainties so tightly that there's no space between them. Their minds are full of sharp edges, like a maze of swords and knives. If you try to squeeze in, challenge any of their truths, no matter how false they are? It's far easier for them to shred *you* than to turn the blades on themselves."

"Damn," Wash muttered.

AJ turned in the circle of Wash's arms. "I've never possessed a child before. Her mind might not be as jagged and crystalized, but what if I can't escape? There's no master to yank me back should anything go wrong." He swallowed. *Can I confess this? My deepest fear?* But when he gazed into Wash's bottomless dark eyes, he knew Wash might be the only person he *could* tell. "What if I'm tempted to stay this time?" he whispered.

"In the first place" —Wash kissed AJ's forehead—"she's a pre-pubescent human girl. I doubt she's got a power base that could launch an evil empire, so she's probably a really lousy choice for permanent possession. Unless you're just a really incompetent demon."

AJ choked on a laugh. "Many of my masters have uttered rather forceful complaints to that effect. They expected someone more fearsome than a librarian, and an assistant one at that."

"More fools they. In the second place, you don't have a master, but you do have a tether." He took AJ's hand and placed it on his chest. "To me. And I'll keep you safe. I promise."

Chapter Seven

AJ stood at the end of the girl's bed, Wash a warm, solid presence at his back, while Ky and Dr. Mori conferred in the corner. At a murmured comment from Dr. Mori, Ky left the room, then returned, wheeling a cart with a full exorcism kit.

AJ swallowed. They might claim they trusted him to eject when his task was complete, but they were clearly taking no chances. In a way, that made him more confident. If he succumbed to temptation, despite Wash's assurances to the contrary, they'd do what was necessary. They'd prevent him from turning into a monster.

"Hey." Wash put his hand on AJ's waist as Ky began placing wrist-thick white candles at the room's cardinal points. The scent of beeswax and angelica joined the harsh tang of hand sanitizer and ozone. "You'll be fine. I'll be right here, holding your hand."

"You can't. When I possess someone, I go completely astral. My physical body will vanish."

Wash blinked. "Ooookay. Glad you said so. Otherwise I might have had a panic attack of my own."

"Watch her hands though." At present, they were limp, fingers slightly curled toward her palms. "When I'm fully in possession, I'll make this signal." AJ held up his right hand, the index and middle fingers extended close together. "When I'm ready to eject, I'll do this." He folded his fingers into a fist and stuck out his thumb.

Wash smiled. "Hitching a ride?"

"You could say that."

Dr. Mori moved to the bedside and nodded to AJ. "Whenever you're ready."

AJ swallowed against a lump the size of his fist. Other than his last master, who'd practically invited him in, he'd never even considered possessing someone on his own. Maybe he couldn't, not without the threat of punishment or the hope of reward. Then he looked at the little girl. *She deserves to be happy. She deserves a life.* Surely that was incentive enough.

But first…

He turned to Wash, cupping the back of his neck. He leaned forward and murmured, "Auni-jel-Chandu."

Wash gasped, one hand going to his chest as the knowledge ignited in his *calon,* burning along the tether from AJ's. "How… What…"

"My true name. Now you have a tether to me as I have one to you." Sure enough, when AJ shifted his vision to the astral, a second cord had joined the first, blue-green twining with red-gold.

Then he turned to the girl. And dove.

Wash cried out, a guttural noise from deep in his soul, because AJ was suddenly gone, his glasses falling onto the bed as his scrubs crumpled to the floor. *Don't panic. Don't panic. He warned you how it would be.* Wash took a deep breath, and the fullness, the *rightness* in his chest, directly below his heart where his *calon* lived, reassured him. AJ was still with him, even if he wasn't precisely *with* him.

He kept a close watch on the patient, and sure enough —

"There!" He pointed at her tiny hand, two fingers unfurling from a loose fist. "He's in."

Behind the girl's eyelids, her eyes started to move as if she'd shifted into REM sleep.

"That's definitely a change," Dr. Mori said.

Wash frowned at her tone of grudging surprise. "Didn't you expect it?"

She raised an eyebrow. "My dear Mr. Hernández, have *you* ever witnessed a demonic possession?"

"No."

"Neither have I. Neither has anyone in recent memory. It's gone out of fashion. People these days have enough license to indulge in poor behavior without the need to shift the blame onto an opportunistic devil. Access to goods has increased as well. It's far easier to order something online than to go to the trouble of summoning a demon and inserting a rather high-maintenance middleman into the equation."

Wash rubbed his chest. "So why did you make him do it?"

She tilted her head, regarding the patient with somewhat less detachment than he was used to seeing from her. "Frankly, we were out of options. And because of the previous neglect, Amber's strength is failing rapidly."

"Amber. That's her name?"

"Yes. Amber Thompkins." She studied him, her gaze flicking from his face to his chest. "Is something the matter? Do you have heartburn?"

"What?" Wash winced at a sharp pain under his sternum which felt remarkably like a burn, although not of the acid reflux variety. "No. Just a little discomfort. I'm fi—" He gaped, words gone, breath gone, pain spearing him like a knife. Sweat broke out on his forehead and upper lip and prickled along his spine. "Something's wrong," he wheezed.

"Ky!" Dr. Mori barked. "Get the silver athame. Light the candles."

With Zuri on his shoulder, Ky called flame to the candle in the north and west quadrants. But somehow, Wash knew that was wrong. "No!" The candles snuffed out immediately, followed by Ky's curse and Zuri's furious squawk. "That's not how to do it. Don't *force* him. This isn't something wrong with Amber." He gasped again, beginning to shiver, hunching over as if a vast, amorphous beast hovered overhead, toothed maw gaping. "Something's wrong with AJ."

"Then we should definitely begin the exorcism to pull him out. If he were to take command—"

"Shut up!" Wash was yelling at a doctor, but he couldn't be bothered with what it would do to his career. "He's not like that. This has to be because of something he found. Something that's—" He ducked, expecting harpy claws to rake his scalp—but nothing was there. Just the sub-audible hum of the fluorescent lights, the beep of the heart monitor, and Ky's murmured reassurance to Zuri. "Whatever's wrong with Amber is affecting him too. He needs help." *And I'm the only one who can give it.* "Turn out the lights," Wash snapped. "Do you *want* to blind him when he gets back?" *And he'll get back, hale and whole. He will. I won't allow anything less.*

Wash retrieved AJ's glasses and tucked them into his shirt pocket. Then he gripped the bed rail, forcing himself to stay in place when he wanted nothing more than to find the nearest deep hole and hide in it for the next millennium.

Except he didn't want that. Did he? *No, these aren't my feelings. They're AJ's. He's terrified.*

Wash's throat clogged, something pushing up from his belly, squeezing his lungs. "Come back!" The words burst out of his mouth. "Don't leave me!"

Ky grabbed his elbow. "Easy, there. I don't think shouting at him will do the trick."

"Those... weren't..." Wash panted, trying to keep another cry bottled up. "*My* words."

"They sure as hells weren't mine. Whose— Hold up." Ky peered into Wash's face, his fingers tightening to the point of pain. "Your eyes are glowing like his did. What in blazes have you done?"

"Nothing." But that was about to change. Wash gripped the rail harder, closing his eyes and calling on the link he and AJ had forged in that supply room with kisses and promises and magic. On the connection they'd felt from the first moment they'd met. On the truth of AJ's name, nestling deep in Wash's heart. Wash opened his eyes and looked down. A braided cord, red-gold and green-blue, shimmered faintly in the air between his chest and the girl in the bed.

"What in the name of the triple goddess is *that*?" Ky muttered.

Wash ignored him. *It's time, Auni-jel-Chandu. Come back to me. Come home.* He found a place inside him, a place he'd never thought to touch, that let him grab onto that astral tether and *pull*.

Suddenly the room was overfull of demon wings, and AJ was standing at the foot of the bed, precisely where he'd last been, once again naked, just as Wash had first seen him. AJ's eyes rolled back, and he started to crumple but Wash was there, catching him, cradling him, lowering him, limp-winged, to the floor.

"It's okay, love. You're back. You're safe." He fumbled AJ's glasses out of his scrub pocket, but with one arm trapped under AJ's body, he couldn't unfold them. "Shit."

"Allow me." Dr. Mori took the spectacles and placed them gently on AJ's nose as Ky covered his body with a sheet.

"AJ?" Wash smoothed AJ's rumpled curls off his forehead. "Can you hear me?"

AJ's eyelids fluttered, and his gaze snapped to Wash's. His eyes blazed red. He pointed at Dr. Mori, but nothing emerged from his mouth but a croak.

Wash glanced between AJ and Doctor Mori, bewildered. "You need the doctor to do something?"

AJ shook his head, his forehead furrowed, whether with pain or frustration, Wash couldn't tell. He pointed more insistently.

"I don't know what you—"

"Pen," AJ wheezed.

Wash glanced at Dr. Mori. Sure enough, she was holding a pen in her hand. He snapped his fingers, motioning for her to hand it over. *First, I yell at her. Then I snap my fingers at her. I'm so fired.*

But she handed it over, along with a clipboard holding a legal pad. Wash ripped off a page of her notes and tossed it aside, then placed the pen and clipboard in AJ's trembling hands.

"Whoa," Ky murmured. "Supersonic artwork. Impressive. It's like a time-lapse without the lapse."

Because AJ's hand was barely visible, it was moving so rapidly. A drawing, remarkable in its minute detail, appeared as if by magic on the yellow paper. *D'oh. That's because it is magic. AJ's magic.*

Ky leaned over, peering at the picture. On his shoulder, Zuri cocked her head, then turned her back, feathers fluffed in disgust. "A cat? What does a cat have to do with anything? If this is an anaphylactic response, I've never seen one this severe when the allergen trigger isn't present."

"Not... allergic." AJ let the pen clatter to the floor, all the tension leaving his body as he slumped in Wash's arms. "Familiar."

Although it was probably self-indulgent of him, AJ nestled against Wash, letting Wash's touch, his presence, his warmth, ground him in his body once more. *I probably should have warned them about the post-possession recovery period.* But it hadn't occurred to him. His magician masters had never cared, and he'd been left to himself to mend as best he could—at least until they wanted something more from him.

He'd certainly never gotten tenderness.

"Here." Wash held a cup to AJ's lips. "Drink this. It might help with the shock."

"Shock?" But AJ took a sip of the beverage, warm and sweet.

"You've got the symptoms." Wash's smile was fond and did more than the drink to replenish AJ's reserves.

"You know," Ky drawled, "this looks an awful lot like familiar aftercare."

Wash frowned at him. "Shut up." When he turned back to AJ, though, his expression smoothed again. "Do you feel up to a little more explanation?"

"Yes." AJ tried to sit up, but Wash kept him anchored against his chest. AJ retracted his wings so he could get closer. *Who cares if it's self-indulgent?* "She needs her familiar."

"You mean this is bond-trauma?" Ky hunkered down in front of them, Dr. Mori at his back. "But that's impossible. Even if she'd been identified as a witch—"

"She definitely has a *calon*," AJ said, then took another sip of the beverage. "However, it's weakening. Quickly."

"She's too young," Ky said. "Familiars never bond with witches until they're adults. We never even considered bond-trauma as a cause."

AJ drained the cup, then cradled it against his chest. "Nevertheless, she's got a familiar. A cat. She's had it for several years, but whoever packed her off to foster care didn't bring it along." AJ couldn't help his accusing glare at the doctor. "She begged them to, but they didn't pay any attention."

Dr. Mori raised an eyebrow. "You needn't glare at me. Since she hadn't been identified as a supe, human social services would have caught the case. They wouldn't have realized the physical importance of the cat, although they might have considered the psychological impact." Her voice held a distinctly sharp edge. "Although even supe authorities might not have listened. The idea that a familiar would bond with a child this young..." She shook her head. "Well, familiars make their own rules. Perhaps this one was responding to the neglect in Amber's case. Giving her the nurture and companionship that her parents failed to provide." She nodded at Ky. "Retrieve the cat and bring it here."

Zuri muttered something uncomplimentary as Ky stood. "Where's her previous home?"

Dr. Mori grabbed the chart and flipped through the pages. "It doesn't say. The foster parents didn't know."

Ky ran a hand through his hair. "Well, shit. How are we supposed to find a cat somewhere in the state of Oregon when we don't even know where to start?"

AJ struggled out of Wash's embrace, although not without regret. "I can find it."

Everyone looked at him as if he'd just announced a plot to take over the supe council.

"How?" Dr. Mori asked.

"When I possess someone—" He gulped, the memories of so many other possessions threatening to swamp him. *But this one is different. This one is to help someone, not for ambition, or power, or wealth.* "When I possess someone, I retain something of their essence, the things that are important to them."

"Like you retain information from books?" Wash asked, stroking AJ's face with a tender smile.

"Exactly." AJ tapped his chest. "Her connection with the cat is the most important thing in her life, so I can still feel its pull. And the cat is here." Zuri squawked. "Well not *here*-here. But close."

Ky slapped his forehead. "Of course. We're talking about a familiar, not a normal cat. She's probably stalking through the St. Stupid's corridors as we speak." He stroked Zuri's head with the tip of a finger. "I know cats aren't your favorite, but could you find her, please, and bring her here?"

Zuri rustled her wings irritably, but then launched herself off Ky's shoulder and winged out the door.

"While she's doing that—" Ky stared down at Wash and AJ. "Maybe you two could tell me what's going on."

Wash grabbed AJ's hand. "None of your business."

Ky snorted. "I'm not talking about your love life. But this here?" He gestured between Wash and AJ. "The matching sets of glowing eyes? An arcane link between you that's bright enough for me to see even without Zuri's help?" He nudged Wash with a toe. "Not to mention that you, dear brother, who've never bespelled so much as a safety match, neutralized my fire magic like a freaking senior magister. So I ask again. What's going on?"

AJ struggled to his feet, clutching the sheet around his middle. "It was my fault. I didn't realize—"

"Hold on." Wash jumped up and gripped AJ's shoulders. "This isn't a one-sided thing. You didn't force a connection on me, just as I didn't force you to give me your name."

"Wait a moment." Dr. Mori nudged Ky aside. "Mr. Hernández, are you saying that you've formed the equivalent of a familiar bond with a *demon*? A *consensual* bond?"

Wash glanced at AJ. "Yeah. I guess I have. We were actually on our way to talk to you about severing it before we got sidetracked."

AJ grabbed Wash's hand. "I don't want to sever it."

Wash smiled wryly. "Neither do I."

"Then—"

A distant squawk heralded the entrance of a fluffy calico cat that AJ recognized all too well. She glared around at all of them as if they were personally responsible for her troubles—or rather, the troubles of her tiny witch—flicked her tail twice, then stalked over to leap gracefully onto the bed and curl up against Amber's stomach. Purring loudly enough to drown out the whir of machinery, she butted her head under one little hand.

Amber's fingers twitched. Then sank into the familiar's fur.

Dr. Mori's eyebrows disappeared under her bangs. "Yes. Well, I think we've run into more than one situation today that challenges some long-held assumptions. Mr. Hernández, AJ—I will expect you in my office the first thing tomorrow to discuss how this new… *partnership*… might benefit the St. Stupid's diagnostic medicine department. In the meantime, if you don't mind vacating the room, I need to attend to this patient."

AJ let Wash lead him out of the room. Once they were in the corridor, Wash grabbed him around the middle and danced him in a circle, winding the sheet around both their legs, nearly pulling it out of AJ's grip.

"I can't believe it." He stroked AJ's cheek, then kissed him softly on the lips. "Despite my malformed calon, I'm now an active witch. All because of you."

AJ cupped Wash's jaw. "Your calon isn't malformed. It's formed perfectly. For me." Then AJ remembered Amber's misery and desolation at being separated from her cat. "Does this mean you have to stick with me or you'll suffer the way Amber did? Have I forced you after all, because you can't do spellcraft without me?"

Wash shrugged. "I doubt it. Zuri isn't always with Ky, and he doesn't suffer any ill effects. Besides, Amber's a kid, and she was in a shitty situation. I'm an adult, and I've got no complaints about my life, especially now." His grin faded. "But if you want to keep this as a strictly, uh, business relationship..."

AJ's heart sank. "Is that what you want?"

"Hells no. Even if we didn't have this connection"—he gestured between the location of his own calon and AJ's—"we have this one." He kissed AJ softly. "Don't we?"

AJ nodded, his heart lifting so high and fast he could swear it had wings of its own. "We do. I intend to hold on to you with all eight arms, if necessary. For as long as you want me."

"I'm pretty sure that's gonna be forever." Wash glanced down at the sheet which was making a break for the floor and chuckled. "If we make a habit of diagnostic possessions, St. Stupid's is gonna need a bigger scrubs budget."

"Oh, I don't know." AJ wound his arms around Wash's neck. "You're a witch. I bet you can figure out how to bespell scrubs for the astral, the way Dr. Mori's pants accommodate her tails."

"Maybe. Though I've gotta say, this post-possession wardrobe of yours has a *lot* going for it." Wash nuzzled AJ's neck below his ear, making him shiver. "What do you say we head upstairs? Possess your bed for a while? Take a few... measurements?" He pulled back, the glint in his eyes decidedly wicked. "Strictly for science, of course."

AJ kissed him again. "That's one type of possession I won't object to in the least."

About Witch Under Wraps

When supernatural secrets collide, it'll take more than coffee to brew the perfect love.

When Ky Hernández bonded with his familiar, Zuri, his life changed forever. Their connection turned him into a practicing witch and led him to his calling as a medimagical professional. However, it totally tanked his love life—what guy would settle for eternal second place behind a parrot? So Ky keeps his witchy nature under wraps and sticks to hookups with humans, which can never go anywhere. But the mouthwatering barista at the coffee shop next door makes him thirst for more than a caffeine fix.

The charms Ewan Jones uses to appear human are inconvenient, disorienting, and . . . necessary. Ewan and his siblings are achubyddion, metaphysical healers whose powers are coveted by unscrupulous supernatural beings. And let's face it: all supes are unscrupulous, given the right incentive. He's grateful for the protections that hide his little family, and for the barista job that keeps them housed and fed. He's just so lonely. And his regular, Ky, the super-hot, commitment-averse EMT, seems like the perfect candidate for a one-night shot at intimacy. After all, humans are no threat.

It takes a clumsy coffee shop intern, a mysterious werewolf epidemic, and one snarky parrot to unravel their pasts—and give them a chance at a future.

a message from

ej

Dear Reader,

Thank you so much for reading *Possession in Session* in this exclusive paperback format. I'm so happy you've taken this journey with me! I'd be immensely grateful if you'd take a moment to leave a review at any site you use for reviews. Believe me, reviews make an *enormous* difference to the health and well-being of books (and not incidentally, to their associated authors!).

If you'd like to catch Wash's brother Ky's romance as assisted (hindered?) by Zuri, it's all there in *Witch Under Wraps*, along with guest appearances by Wash and AJ.

Pop on over to my website, https://ejrussell.com, for all the deets on my books—my paranormal rom-coms and mysteries, my contemporary romances, and my one lone historical. If you're an audio fan, you can find the audio scoop there too. *Witch Under Wraps*, for instance, is narrated by the wonderful Greg Boudreaux. (The QR code below will get you there with your smartphone camera or other code reader.)

Would you like exclusive content and ARC giveaways, not to mention gratuitous dance videos? Then I'd love for you to join me in E.J. Russell's Reality Optional, my Facebook fan group (https://facebook.com/groups/reality.optional). My newsletter is the place to get the latest dish on new releases, sales, and more. I promise I only send one out when I've got…well…news. You can subscribe here: https://ejrussell.com/newsletter. (And BTW, my newsletter subscribers get the ebook version of *Possession in Session* for free.)

All my best,
—E

Also by
ej

Paranormal Romance
Mythmatched Universe
Fae Out of Water Trilogy
Cutie and the Beast
The Druid Next Door
Bad Boy's Bard

Supernatural Selection Trilogy
Single White Incubus
Vampire With Benefits
Demon on the Down-Low

Other Mythmatched Romances
Howling on Hold
Possession in Session
Witch Under Wraps
Cursed is the Worst
The Skinny on Djinni
Assassin by Accident (part of Carnival of Mysteries)

Quest Investigations Mysteries
Five Dead Herrings
The Hound of the Burgervilles
The Lady Under the Lake
Death on Denial

At Odds with the Gods (A Mythmatched/Purgatory Playhouse crossover)

Mythmatchedlets (Mythmatched companion stories, free to newsletter subscribers in ebook form, collected in one paperback volume: *Second First Date, Rusty's Really Bad Day, First Flight, Getting the Band Together, Purgatory Postscript, A Very Quest Solstice*)

Magic Emporium Series (shared world)
Purgatory Playhouse

Enchanted Occasions Series
Best Beast
Nudging Fate
Devouring Flame

Ghost Townies Series
Ghostridden

Legend Tripping Series
Stumptown Spirits
Wolf's Clothing

Art Medium Series
The Artist's Touch
Tested in Fire
Art Medium: The Complete Collection (omnibus edition)

Royal Powers Series (shared world)
Duking It Out

Duke the Hall
King's Ex

Science Fiction
Sun, Moon, and Stars Series
Partnership
Principles

Interdimensional Time Bureau
Monster Till Midnight

Historical Romance
Silent Sin

Contemporary Romance
Camera Shy
Summer Kitchen
The Thomas Flair
Mystic Man
For a Good Time, Call… (A Bluewater Bay novel, with
Anne Tenino)

Christmas Kisses (holiday shorts)
The Probability of Mistletoe
An Everyday Hero
A Swants Soiree

Geeklandia Series
The Boyfriend Algorithm (M/F)
Clickbait

Writing as Nelle Heran

(traditional cozy mystery)

Crafty Sleuth Series (with C.K. Eastland)
Die Cut
Mixed Media
Found Objects (*coming soon*)

About the
Author

E.J. Russell (she/her), author of the award-winning Mythmatched paranormal romance series, writes LGBTQ+ romance and mystery in a rainbow of flavors. Count on high snark, low angst, and happy endings.

Reality? Eh, not so much.

She's married to Curmudgeonly Husband, a man who cares even less about sports than she does. Luckily, C.H. also loves to cook, or all three of their children (Lovely Daughter and Darling Sons A and B) would have survived on nothing but Cheerios, beef jerky, and Satsuma mandarins (the extent of E.J.'s culinary skill set).

E.J. also writes traditional cozy mystery as Nelle Heran. She lives in rural Oregon, enjoys visits from her wonderful adult children, and indulges in good books, red wine, and the occasional hyperbole.

News & Social Media:
Website: https://ejrussell.com
Newsletter: https://ejrussell.com/newsletter

Acknowledgements

I owe big thanks to L.C. Chase for the adorable cover; to Meg DesCamp and Hana Katen (my Lovely Daughter) for editing and proofing; to my family (Jim, Hana, Nick, Ross, and Billy) for support and encouragement; and to my awesome PA, NOLAKim, for keeping me from being a *total* recluse.

And, always and forever, thank you to my readers for accompanying me on this journey. You're the reason I can continue to follow my heart, and I appreciate you more than I can say.